FROM YOU & ME TO US

HANSIKA PARMAR

FROM YOU & ME TO US

ISBN: 978-93-94759-37-4

Brown Page Publication
Regd. Under MSME ACT 2016

Brown Page Publication

29A Faizupur Khadar, Tigaon 90,
Ballabgarh,Faridabad,Haryana-121101
Ph - +91-7428778978

To the person I see when I close my eyes

ACKNOWLEDGEMENT

Thanking someone to support you has been one of the most common acknowledgements. But for this I would like to thank my inspiration who has not only done things for me which I can not explain and also been the person I don't wanna hide writing about.

You are not that bad. I can say you're bearable but I would definitely say this work would not have existed if I had not got you when I did. So thank you.

YOU

You are not what others see you as. You are an entertainer, a kind friend, a hardworking employee, a patriot, a cricket lover and most of all a great listener. I have never seen somebody this calm my entire life. Falling in love with you was easy but it would not have been as successful as I say it is if you would not have been the most understanding, supportive and hilarious.

You have seen me as I am and took it under your protection which I dare say should be the rest of my life.

So here I am writing all about you. I do not care what you've been through but I know I wouldn't die without being a part of what you're going through.

CRICKET

It's not just a game
It's a string to the religions
It's the music in all the anthems
And the joy behind the tears

It's the reason for playing
And realizing the unity hidden
It's all from the players
But all for the nations

It's been along for years
And still is a moment with peers
It's not just the game of cricket
It's your memory with your dears

A BOY

I saw all the stories
I sang all the songs
I dreamt her being pretty
And i saw him being strong

I saw what she was
And what she was gonna become
I saw him in a shadow black
And her being the white so pure

But i don't get this point
Why only bad guys get what they want
What about the girls in black
Can't someone cut them some slack

Get them a guy with the cutest of smile
The one who's known to be purest of white
A guys who makes her perfectly smile
A boy who calls her "perfectly mine"

THAT SUIT

I saw him enter
In that navy blue suit
His walk was like the winter
That tied my eyes in it

The room was filled with humor
And some old fake stories
I hope when we talk here
You share what is real

It's not just that the suit
Took all of my soul
It's just that he looks so stunning
My heart cant get away too soon

Fly me to the moon
With these shoulders and that height
I won't mind being your today
And hope you won't leave tonight

I'm still on other side of the room
And i know you've just entered
But what to do of my sight
That dreams about you in that suit.

PROUD

He looks out the window
To look back in his life
He's seen all things too early
People say he's too mature

He's been with girls who are pretty
And with girls who are tall
But all his life what he could be
Was alone at back and proud

SAME MISTAKES

He was still the sun back then
Tied up into some wrong
He was lost in his own eyes
Like eclipse on the sun

He learnt things the hard way
And lost things that he want
He learnt it all the hard way
That things are meant to be gone

He lost his friends and got alone
Won't say as such because he's not a poem
He is happy as he has been before
Just the past has some open shores

He took his time to get in line
And understand what he wants
He knew he wont be that dumb again
To make the same mistakes again.

FOOD AND YOU

Your eyes sparkle when I talk about a food
Well I hope you're not cheating on me
Your mind is as sharp as the knife you love
And all I think about the pasta that you cook
You've been the person to work on you dreams
And made me think about your reaction to things
Your lips are gifted with the perfect of smiles
Which can take my everything as a nickel of time
We have been through so much individually
I can not wait to do the rest together
I can't wait to eat my pizza with you
When you realize that I can not eat more than this
It's not all that I miss
But I think it's enough for now.

SUN

I woke up to see your face
I wished it true it wasn't a disgrace
He's hiding behind the clouds
To see me smile about

But the clouds seem to be a bad crowd
Hiding him from all
But still sharing him so tall
He grins when I come out
And look for him without a doubt

He wants me but he's shy
He can't say his moon bye bye

He tells our stories to all
Even though I'm not so tall
He loves me more than anything
Coz I have loved his season for all.

HIS SCENT

A dash of his nature
Not dull but not too fresh
Some bits of the spice
Like he sounds when he's right

Some parts of the red
Bold as he is when sad
A little of the lemon
Which is too much on the onion

I smelled something different once
A scent which wasn't his to begun
But I forgot i hugged him all night
My scent must have seen the light

ME

WANTS

Many times this question comes to mind…

What do you want from life???

All of us have different answers but, I will share mine with a poem

Wants

What do you want from life?

A house of my own

A job to earn enough

A guy to fall for everyday

And a friend to cry my day

My love for nature has never been hidden by me as well as my work. Since I have started writing, I have always been inspired by the beauty of the sky, including all its parts; Clouds, The Sun, Stars and its creations. When we talk about me it includes all the parts of me in love with the nature around me.

COTTON BALLS

It was when i was on ride
I saw the thing you designed
A beauty in all the chaos
A shadow to all the light

I've loved your shapes
Since the beginning of time
I like your pace coz
It feels like I'm following the sunshine

You're a provider for what we need
A drop of rain in the drought
You're the pureness of whites
And look as some common cotton balls

THE PLACE

Here i am
And all these flowers around me
The lilies whirring the wind around
And the daisies standing to hear the sound
The tulips to remind you the strength you need
And the roses to tell you that you've promises to keep
Some small flowers whose name I don't know
But i promise they have all the colors i know
Blue, green, orange and pink
Think of the colors you'll forget what you think
All of them made the garden unique
But the sunflower got me to think
It showed me how much I'll miss you at night
Coz you're my sun and I can't follow you if not for the
light.

WHEN THE SKY TALKS

★☽

I went upstairs to look the sky
When there is not much of day
I went upstairs to sing so light
The bright star shines again

I saw that wind comb through my hair
And watched it talk to me
Through narrows whooshes of sweetheart songs
And pushed me there again

I remembered us unbroken love
Talks all so smooth so brave
We kept it low for so much long
Now there's not much to say

This night brought light into my mind
I sang and cried again
If time comes soon we see the noon
I hope you're still not there

GALAXY

Here she is
Her hair as wet as
The stars are falling
Her smile like
The crescent crawling
Her walk like
The revolutions to see
And her existence
Is just like the Milky Way Galaxy

THE MOON

The moon just keeps on staring me
Like the smile of his telling me
The things that are awaited for me
To live my life in his shadow

Well he says he won't be around that much
Even though he doesn't have responsibilities as such
He just likes to wander around
With something he calls as his cloud

It's his secret he won't accept in real
That I am his own miracle
Coz he nobody else is able to get him right
Its like I get him as if I'm his child

He told me to stay away from stars
Coz they lie and cheat with blinking skies
So I got myself The Sun so bright
That the moon said fine fine fine...

He told me not to disrespect The Sun
He's the god and I am just a nun
Well I kept a secret from him too
He didn't knew that The Sun is in love with me too

AURORA

I think I saw her
The goddess of dawn
In her chariot
Welcoming her sibling

Calling for Sol and
Biding Luna adieu
Looking for her lover
In the greenest of plains

Her hair mystical
Her eyes magical
Her love so sure
But blind for him pure

Watched her moving around
She tried not to make a sound
But how to miss
Such a bliss
When you see a goddess
Who had caught herself
In the bidding of love

I have loved my parents since forever but nothing comes before my mother.

MOTHER❤

She's got the grace
Of a fallen angel
She's got the smile
Like a cloud's silver line
She's got the love
More than anyone above
She has the magic
All the world combined
She's not yours
She's mine
Her care has the power
To heal all wounds
She's not just my lover
She's my mother

PARENTS

You see them move
You hold their groove
You climb them up
You push them down

You shout their names
You call their blames
You hide what's right
They tell you're bright

Their love isn't a lie
You can't imagine why
You can never gain your talents
Without the love of your parents

You can not see the goodness of love without failing once and that is what makes you the person you wanna be when you find the right one. So to some of my mistakes as well.

OVER YOU

I'm Happy you've got some new friends
I've seen how hard it has been
I hope you get what you become
I think I'll be over you now

I met new friends and old
I cleansed all the dead souls
I feared facing alone
But i know I'm over you now

It's good to feel alone
Coz sometimes it's all you own
Feels like another soul
Just left your body blown

A HOPELESS ROMANTIC

I am a hopeless romantic
Waiting for the chase to begin
I am just a wanderer in love
Trying to find what I believe in

It's said that I've broken hearts
It's said that I've dated a lot
But what difference does it make
If I date once you say try again

It's not about who you choose
It's all about what you want
It's about getting the love that you deserve
And finding a same romantic you want

DAUGHTER OF THE WAR

She floats like a dream,
Before she sinks under,
Carrying in her folds,
The dying cries of the soldiers...

The sorrow of their widows
And the deaths of their lovers
The emptiness that lies
In the grounds of their coven

She has the power of their hearts
Which gives her voice the strength
To fulfill her life with no regrets
And live her life with full health

She saw every bit too early
Young mind which saw the war
Young heart which cried everyday
To the death of those she abhor

She has got the guts to fight alone
And the mind to beat them all
She is the daughter of the war
And the sister of them all

PRIEST

She rises from the ashes,
Donning infinite avatars,
Sending the vile searching for cover,
And begging for mercy are the stars

They've been hiding all around
Trying to find who is the one
They've been burning to the ground
But in the ashes she returns

Her mind has nothing hard to hide
She came here ready for a fight
She called herself not the god
Just a priest of a sort.

NEGATIVES

You've fallen again
He's not perfect
He's not a priest
But he's yours

You've fallen again
He's not been so good
He's not what you thought
He's just better

You've fallen again
You don't deserve him
You shouldn't trust him
Don't do this again
Don't fall in prey again
Trust your instinct I'll say
Don't just be negative i'll say

USED TO

I got used to trying again
I got used to falling again
I saw what life hadn't given me
I got used to accepting again

Faced the changes meant for me
Made the cakes without the cream
Followed my path to meet you here
I got used to loving you dear

I see all the things we do
I've got used to falling for you
Now the only thing that scared me
Is if you get used to not being with me

FEEL

I don't know if I can make your heart to change
So I'll write a better song to make it rain
I can see the light that you try to make it hide
They tell me that you have had a lot to fight
I hope this just makes you feel alive
I hope this just makes you feel tonight

I saw you there in the park with all alone
I came by to see if you can see me go
But your mind was somewhere else aside
Someplace where i didn't seem to walk in light
So i just hope this makes you feel alive
I just hope this makes you feel tonight

I'll be there when the day seems to be gone
And the night is crawling up along its own
And you see me with the spark inside
And we can have some time tonight
So i just hope this makes you feel alive
And I just hope this makes you feel tonight.

US

How do you get to know that the person is someone you want to spend your life with. Someone who is gonna be there and is going to adjust according to your habits. Well it all just starts with the talk and the getting to know part. And then comes the kiss.

A KISS

Talked about the day
Had nothing else to say
Well we went to that quiet place
To have a kiss to replace

A kiss so strong it broke all chords
A kiss so long it came along
A kiss to miss all secrets gone
A kiss which said you're not alone

His lips now only craved for her taste
Her smile made him want it again
They kissed so sweet the flowers bloomed
She smelled like him and he liked the moon.

THE MOONLIGHT

Sitting under the moonlight
He told me what he felt like
When i had my head on his shoulder
And my hand on his thigh

We went to a lot of places
With known and unknown faces
All that was needed to survive
Was our time in the moonlight

A time came when he told her his heart
She said she knew it from the start
It's not just a broken part
I love you is just the start

IMAGINATION

If imagination had a camera
It would've seen the fire in my heart
Turning Itself into a sunset
Just to make it more acceptable

If imagination had a camera
It would've clicked my success
And given the world a glimpse of the future
To brace themselves for it

If imagination had a camera
I would've made myself a perfect life
Which would have proof of each of Its moments
And I would make sure it's with you.

THAT WAY

I saw him smile
Like quarter of a mile
I saw him live on his life
Trying not to be on his way

I saw him play
Harness all the anger within
All that memories rushed from within
And i felt like i should talk to him again

Stopped my thoughts
And restarted my playlist
It's better to be away
And stay that way

YOUR MOON

You've been with me
With your white light
Which shines so bright
Like that sun right above me.

Give a part of it to me
Give me my existence
Just make me follow you all around
All is want is to be your moon profound

THE WINDOW

A window of tears
And unbroken peers
A sill full of elbows
Filled to fit on the edges
A time full of words
And letters and stories
A noise of the call
Made to call out his name
Just to watch him smile
And say you goodbye
A place made to breathe
In an unhappy reel
It's not just a window for breezes
It's a glass where time freezes

LOVE TO DESERVE

Hidden in the soul
Of your unwanted body
Lies the things that you feel
About you and me
We both seem alive
But mostly dead inside
And smile a little
Just to prove the presence

Let's run off one day
To a new place to stay
And have all the love
That you and I deserve

SEE…

It's when you see his eyes
You realize
What is the love that you wanted
And the smile that made you smile
The words you always wanted to hear
And the hands you always wanted to hold
It's when his arms hold you tight
You realize
That's all of what you always wanted to be

IT'S EASY

It's easy with him
I don't know how it is
I find it hard to believe
That It's too easy to fall in love

Have had your days
When it isn't what you want
But then he came to overcome
All the things that i didn't want

He's cute he's smart
But he's not alone
I think that's the reason
I love him the most

CROWD

You see the crowd
All eyes are on you
And all you can think of
Is getting back to him

Dancing in all upbeats
Getting drunk with your girls
There's a guy who asked you
Will you go out with me

She said i have someone
And all she thinks about is him
Only him
I think she loves him

HIS MUSIC

I want us to be together like this
Like It's a rhythm and beat
I wanna become something that's new
Something that's never happened before

I wanna be the one, the only
I want to be something like
Music is to me....everything
It would be something so naive

Naive that makes him crave for it
And he doesn't wanna skip any part
Something that is compatible with his all
And something that isn't meant to fall

WORTH

Is it his smile
Or just his existence
That is enough to take whats mine
Or is it just his eyes
That just doesn't get up from me

Is it just me
Or does he feel the same
The feeling that we get
When we're falling for someone again

His glare is all that i need
To get up and walk all over again
To make the same mistakes i ever did
Coz this time i know it's worth it

Have you ever just fallen in love and had to go for long distance? We have and it would not be wrong to say that it is painful. You don't know what is coming in the future and what is going to happen, you are worried for your career and his part in it. Being in two different countries with different timelines makes it worse. But we are grateful to say that it is working out. Just missing someone is never easy and words have been my only escape.

HERE

I'm sitting alone but he's right here
Sitting beside commenting on my choices
Laughing on my decisions
He's right here helping me take them again

He's been there when you weren't
He's seen things that i hid from him
He's still there i don't know how
But he's still here for me

HE'S MINE

I love him like no one else does
I'm not his mother but won't be much
He's got the face of an angel
But the smile says he's evil
Fair so bright the sun won't shine
Holds me tight until I'm crying
Looks at me like he's lucky alive
To be with me but that's not fine
I've been with people worse and worse
He's been the best and It's not a verse
I know i say it every time
But this time I'll prove it that he'll stay mine

HEAD

My head on his shoulders
Me trying to pull him closer
Laying on the beach
Thinking it all under
Kissing like married
Hugging like one
All i see when i see you
Is my head on your chest
Forever

I KNOW

I know you miss me
When you wake up alone
I know you miss me
When you're sitting alone
I know you text me
When you can not
I know you'll be the
One to call when you want

I know you'll miss me
At every sunset
And I know you'll see
Me looking at you constant
I know you miss me
When you eat alone
I know you miss me
When you can't say what you want

So don't accept it that's okay
Coz I know you'll miss me anywhere you stay

YOU'RE MY ARTEMIS

Saw you every night
In a different shape
Giving me the light I need
It feels a little poetic
You changing every night
It feels like you're a god

A god of light for the dark
Which makes me miss you all day
I wait for you to come at night
And when you don't
I feel like crying

Your blue eyes meets the sky
To show me what I want
I want here with all my heart
I want you to be my Artemis

DREAM

You're like a fairytale
Entered my life like a dream
Coz all i see when I am with you
Is the life I want with you ahead

I see the things that you've done
And made me feel the princess I've become
You've been my savior and my choice
You've been my music and my voice

I've seen the days that made me miss
The secret place of ours to kiss
With you I'm the one in an open crowd
Coz you're a dream that makes me proud

GOODBYES

We are far away i know
We will talk again for sure
But you're the face that i need
But you're the thing that I'll keep

We talk for hours that feels less
We tried to cover the time we miss
But all these things are fine
Until I have to say to you bye bye

It doesn't happen with all you know
Coz I am never the one to call you know
I know we're not meant to fall
But I won't ever be able to say goodbye on call.

REWARD

One day you'll have it right
That day sun will have the light
He asked me what do you want
When all your wait is gone

When you've seen all the works
To keep your love on terms
You've seen what life has for you
And what is meant to be

When you're asked for the reward
Of your hardships for which you fall
What would you want from god
What could you ask from god? HIM- forever

NEVER LET GO

I make him walk in front
Every time
There's a reason on that front
Only we know that

I walk slow and he knows
So his hand stays back
With the little finger out
Calling out for my left

I hold his finger
With my small hand
And all that I feel is
I should never let go

It has been like that
For months passed away
And it's gonna be the same
Till the days left are nay.

FROM ME TO YOU

Up across the room
There you are
Between all the faces
And after all the glass

From me to you
I want everybody to leave
From me to you
I hate everybody too much

Saw me walk to you
And have small talks
With all the unknown faces
And students from the same class

Walked me to you
I crossed everybody
To talk to you
I skipped everybody

WHITE AND BLACK

You told me i have too many
Whites to wear, but i need more
I can see you've a lot of black
But i won't say coz you I adore

We've been like the colors we like
Something of purest of forms
You're the black and I'm the white
Nothing can be as such pure

We'll keep these colors with us
Cherish the mix of gray forever
Coz white is mine and black is yours
We'll keep it same forever

I'll walk down in white
You'll be waiting in black
Crying in your happy eyes
When you see me in my wedding dress

Then you'll remember I've a lot of whites
And I'll say your black is mine now.

TOGETHER

We're moving ahead... Together
We're staying away... Together
We're falling in love... Together
We're trying to stay... Together
We've felt like this is true... Together
We laughed on the call... Together
We've faced all our problems... Together
We're meant to be found... Together

One day you'll all see
It's with so much of glee
We'll follow each other
And dance around... Together

STAY

Here we are
At the end of a chapter
Waiting for the next one to begin
We don't know how it ends
Nor we know when it does
All I know is…
I wanna be with you

Don't go
Don't stay that away from me
Stay where you belong
My heart and stay there forever.

HOME

Home is what the heart want
A shoulder to cry on
A lil bit of adulation
Too much of compassion

Two arms meant to hug you
Two eyes to share your tears
Two lips to smile and make all better
One life to share with one another

Home is what your smile wants
A chest to sleep when tired
A window with no view... Just you

I MISS YOU

I miss your laugh
I miss your lips maybe
I miss your smile
Coz its all mine
I miss us together
I miss you alone
I miss all the fun
And the recordings
I know you know
What I mean
But what I miss the most
Is your smell at all costs

ONE

I've never been this patient
Never been this calm
Coz I have the most messed up mind
I've done things I regret
And things that i want to forget
But you won't be any of those
Coz you're the cure to all my addictions
And the result of to my prayers
You're what i want to become
And the one that my future holds

LOSE HIM

Found him when I didn't have to
Met him when I didn't meant to
Loved him when i didn't want to
Called him when I didn't had to

Kissed him when I didn't think through
Pissed him just when said I hate you
Loved him when I didn't want to
Missed him when I couldn't lose him

WITH YOU

I feel like i miss you too much
Like my eyes missing my glasses
Coz I can't see clear
And keep tumbling down

I wanna be there when you say
Stuff that people don't care
And i say you always see that in people
When you make a proud face

I love you for that
And all the things to come
But i wanna be there with you
Right now and forever

NEED TO WANT

When you miss someone
You say that you need them
But it's not so easy to say
I don't need you

I don't need you coz
You don't complete me
I am happy as I am and
Willing to stay the same

So here I say
I don't need you
I want you...

I want you for the life left
I want you for the heart theft
I want you to face my problems
With me coz I'm tired of doing it alone

THE THOUGHT

I thought of it today
For the first time
The idea of not being with you
The idea of not waiting for you

It was just for a moment
By the next moment my eyes
Saw nothing coz of the water
Pouring down like fire

I'm not patient i know
But I'm being what I'm not
Coz I know you're the one
That I can not live without

So I'll be patient
Until I go crazy
Coz when I do
I'll be the one who doesn't deserve you

A DREAM TO LIVE

Is it possible to live in a dream
Follow your character until it's true
Or until it's right in front you
Like being a girl hugging you

Yes coz i had dream
Where my arms were around you
Tying you in my life forever
I knew it wasn't real

I knew it wasn't real
But still I wanted to spend
My eternity alone there
Until you come and kiss me up

I knew it wasn't real
Coz I wasn't able to get your scent
Something I've been wanting
Something that feels like for years

I won't cry coz i think that makes me weak
Well I don't mind coz i know you love me too
But crying doesn't change my life
So i won't verify this from you

I'd rather be in my dream
Living a lie until it's gone
Gone when you'll be back to me
Coz I'll get the scent of reality

YOU

I meet a thousand people
And you meet the same number
Yet none of them is like you
But that I can see in them is you

Some don't use right words
Some smell just like I don't want them to
Some smile in the worse
Some cook the pasta good

See… it sucks to stay away
Come back and make me see
That you're the one for me
And be there with your smile and scent
So I can stop to pretend

THE DROUGHT

A drought of life
I'm a barren land
I'm just a grain of sand
Dries up to death
Nearest to what's left
Something that's just not
Something to begin
Weary eyes and gone
Into the wrinkled skin
With a smile not true
Nothing to be seen
Then you came Oh cloud!
With a silver line
Saw my pain, went dark
And all that was left was the rain

RELATIONSHIPS

In this course of life
I have seen and had some\
Could be said I was serious for none
I got to realize when I fell for you

What it is to fall and follow
What is it to get ready to leave
The atrocity called my past
For someone who I want to be with
For someone I want to die with

SEASONAL YEAR

Summers have the prettiest skies
Winters have the coziest whites
Fall is not upset as such
Springs just give me butterflies

I met you before i know
But that fall made me fall for you
The winter i spend with you was the best
With the warmest of hugs and kisses so best

Spring made me cry
I don't know you had to leave, why?
The colors didn't seem the same
The flowers didn't bloom so great

My Summer went in patience
Just a screen to see your face
Waiting for the winter again
Waiting for this fall to end

POSSIBILITY

What would've happened
If I hadn't met you
If I hadn't make you smile
By those small silly deeds of mine

It's a thought
Telling me you are meant to be
Someone who will be mine

It's a possibility
We could've been just friends
But I don't think then too
I would be able to pretend

I know you don't think too much
But it's enough you know I do
How could I've missed this guy
Who was meant to be mine

A YEAR

A year of laughter
A year of love
A year to cherish
Someone I fell for
A year you watching
Me with those piercing eyes
A year you've been calling
My name differently
A year has been since
We called out our love
A year ago I came to know
Our fate could be real

All stories deserve an end to initiate a happy ever after. So does this one, and my heart assures me that my forever will begin soon enough.

OTHER BOOKS

Colors of Life

www.ingramcontent.com/pod-product-compliance
Lightning Source LLC
Chambersburg PA
CBHW062112160726
48282CB00026B/777
9789394759374